SLED RACE MYSTERY

By Maria S. Barbo

Illustrated by Duendes del Sur

Hello Reader — Level 1

ISBN 0-439-44417-9

12 11 10 9 8 7 6 5 4 3   3 4 5 6 7/0

Printed in the U.S.A.
First printing, December 2002

SCHOLASTIC INC.
New York · Toronto · London · Auckland · Sydney
Mexico City · New Delhi · Hong Kong · Buenos Aires

and his friends were having

fun in the .

was the best on his .

was the best on her ice

and made the best

.

What did do best?

Eat!

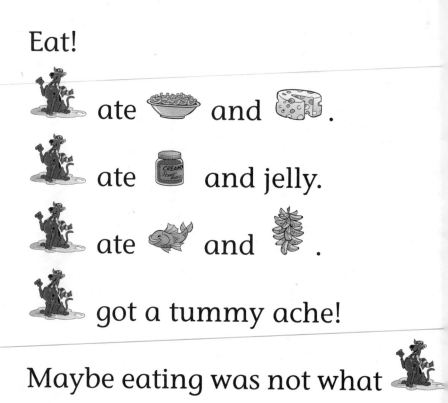

got a tummy ache!

Maybe eating was not what did best.

What *did* do best?

Hide!

Aaaa-ooo!

heard a scary noise.

hid inside a   .

and   were not happy.

Then  saw a sled race.

Each sled was pulled by a dog.

But one dog was missing!

A musher heard a howl.

Then her dog was gone.

"Maybe a thief took my dog!"

said the musher.

"Ruh-roh!"

 was scared.

But wanted to help the .

The loved her .

And the wanted to win a

.

She wanted to have the best

 .

 put on his ice .

put on his and .

looked for the on the

ice.

fell down.

was not the best on ice .

Aaaa-ooo!

"Rikes!" said . "It's the !"

spun on his tail.

lost his .

made fall down.

ran to the top of the .

ran far away from the

He put on some .

looked for the in the

.

Aaaa-ooo!

"The !" said .

went faster.

But was not the best on

crashed into a row of .

 found the !

A did not take the .

The had !

Now, the was too tired to pull the .

 pulled the !

and the won the race.

won a pile of !

The gave her .

"You're the best friend ever, !"

said the .

"Scooby-dooby-doo!"

Did you spot all the picture clues in this Scooby-Doo mystery?

Each picture clue is on a flash card. Ask a grown-up to cut out the flash cards. Then try reading the words on the back of the cards. The pictures will be your clue.

Reading is fun with Scooby-Doo!